Nana Upstairs & Nana Downstairs

Nana Upstairs & Nana Downstairs

story and pictures by
Tomie de Paola

G. P. Putnam's Sons • New York

for my family
— and D.

Text and illustrations copyright © 1973 by Tomie dePaola.
All rights reserved. Published simultaneously in Canada.
Printed in the United States of America.
Library of Congress Catalog Card Number: 72-77965
ISBN 0-399-60787-0 lib. bdg.
ISBN 0-399-21417-8 Tr.
Thirteenth impression

13   15   17   19   20   18   16   14

When Tommy was a little boy, he had
a grandmother and a great-grandmother.
He loved both of them very much.

He and his family would go to visit every Sunday afternoon. His grandmother always seemed to be standing by the big black stove in the kitchen.

His great-grandmother was always in bed upstairs because she was ninety-four years old.

So Tommy called them Nana Downstairs and Nana Upstairs.

Almost every Sunday was the same.
Tommy would run into the house, say
hello to his Grandfather Tom, and Nana
Downstairs and then go up the back
stairway to the bedroom where Nana
Upstairs was.

"Get some candy," Nana Upstairs
would say. And he would open the lid of
the sewing box on the dresser, and there
would be candy mints.

Once Nana Downstairs came into the bedroom and helped Nana Upstairs to the big Morris chair and tied her in so she wouldn't fall out.

"Why will Nana Upstairs fall out?" Tommy asked.

"Because she is ninety-four years old," Nana Downstairs said.

"I'm four years old," Tommy said. "Tie me in a chair too!"

So every Sunday, after he found the candy mints in the sewing box on the dresser, Nana Downstairs would come up the back stairway and tie Nana Upstairs and Tommy in their chairs, and then they would eat their candy and talk.

Nana Upstairs told him about the "Little People."

"Watch out for the fresh one with the red hat with the feather in it. He plays with matches," she said.

"I will," said Tommy.

"There he is!" she said. "Over by the brush and comb. See him?"

Tommy nodded.

When Nana Downstairs had finished
her work by the big black stove and baked
a cake to eat before Tommy went home,
she would come back upstairs.

"Now," Nana Downstairs would say as
she untied Tommy from his chair. "We
must all take our naps."

After their naps, Nana Downstairs
would comb out Nana Upstairs' beautiful
silver-white hair.

Then Nana Downstairs would comb
and brush her own hair.

And she would twist her hair and pin
it up on top of her head.

"Now make the 'cow's tail'!" Tommy
would say.

One time Tommy's older brother came into the bedroom and saw Nana Upstairs with her hair all down around her shoulders, and he ran away.

"She looks like a witch!" he said.

"She does *not!*" Tommy said. "She's beautiful."

"Time for ice cream!" shouted Grandfather Tom. And Tommy and his brother went with him, and sometimes their father and their Uncle Charles down to the ice-cream store.

When they got back, it was time for
Nana Upstairs to have supper, and Tommy
would help carry the tray of milk and
crackers up the back stairway.

Once Tommy's father took movies of
the whole family. He took movies of Nana
Downstairs and Nana Upstairs. And
Tommy stood in the middle.

One morning when Tommy woke up at his own house, his mother came in to talk to him.

"Nana Upstairs died last night," she said.

"What's 'died'?" Tommy asked.

"Died means that Nana Upstairs won't be here anymore," Mother answered.

They went to Tom and Nana Downstairs' house, even though it wasn't Sunday.

Tommy ran up the back stairway before he'd even said hello.
He ran into Nana Upstairs' room.
The bed was empty.

Tommy began to cry.

"Won't she ever come back?" he asked.

"No, dear," Mother said softly. "Except in your memory. She will come back in your memory whenever you think about her."

From then on he called Nana Downstairs just plain Nana.

A few nights later, Tommy woke up
and looked out his bedroom window at the
stars.

All of a sudden, a star fell through the sky. He got up and ran to his mother and father's bedroom.

"I just saw a falling star," he said.
    "Perhaps that was a kiss from Nana
Upstairs," said Mother.

A long time later, when Tommy had grown up, Nana Downstairs was old and in bed just like Nana Upstairs. Then she died too.

And one night, when he looked out his bedroom window, Tommy saw another star fall gently through the sky.

Now you are both Nana Upstairs, he thought.